25¢

ATTACK OF THE ZOMBIES!

ADAPTED BY Alex Harvey
BASED ON THE SCREENPLAY "ONCE BITTEN" WRITTEN BY Casey Alexander,
Chris Mitchell, and Steven Banks

ILLUSTRATED BY Harry Moore

Ready-to-Read

Simon Spotlight/Nickelodeon
New York   London   Toronto   Sydney

Based on the TV series *SpongeBob SquarePants*™ created by Stephen Hillenburg
as seen on Nickelodeon™

SIMON SPOTLIGHT
An imprint of Simon & Schuster Children's Publishing Division
1230 Avenue of the Americas, New York, New York 10020
For information about special discounts for bulk purchases, please contact
Simon & Schuster Sales at 1-866-506-1949 or business@simonandschuster.com
Manufactured in the United States of America
First Edition
2 4 6 8 10 9 7 5 3 1
ISBN 978-1-4424-2087-8

"SpongeBob!" Squidward yelled.
"Will you keep your slimy pet
off my lawn? I am sick of
cleaning up after him."

Squidward started to build
a wooden fence.
"This cheap wood will keep
Gary out!"

Squidward was still yelling about
Gary when the snail suddenly bit him.
"Ahh!" Squidward screamed.
"No, Gary! This is not like you,"
SpongeBob said. "There seems to be
something wrong with him."

"I hope he has had all his shots," Squidward said.

"Oh, of course," SpongeBob replied.

"For rabies?"

"Yes."

"For snail pox?
And Soft Shell Dance?
Bagitis?
Lumpy Bump Trump?"
"Yes, yes, yes, and yes!"
SpongeBob said.

Just then Patrick stopped by.
"How about Mad Snail Disease?"
he asked.

This time SpongeBob could not
say yes.

Patrick looked at Squidward.
"Looks like the rash has started."
Squidward gulped. "Rash?"

"Is your throat sore?"
Patrick asked.

"Uh . . . yes," Squidward said.

"Hmm . . . do you feel like
you are falling?
Does your rib cage feel ticklish?
And your toenails are not trimmed?"

"Well, I, uh . . . ," Squidward started
to say.
"Squidward, that bite will turn you
into . . . a zombie!" Patrick cried.

"SpongeBob, you need to get that snail of yours to a doctor!" Patrick said.

But Gary was gone.

Then Patrick began to shout,
"Ahh! Mad snail on the loose!
If he bites you, you will turn
into a zombie!"

At first no one believed Patrick.
Gary looked too cute to have
Mad Snail Disease.

But when Gary bared his teeth,
everyone screamed.

"Mad Snail Disease is real!"
they shouted.
"I have been bitten by a
mad snail! I am a zombie!"
someone yelled.

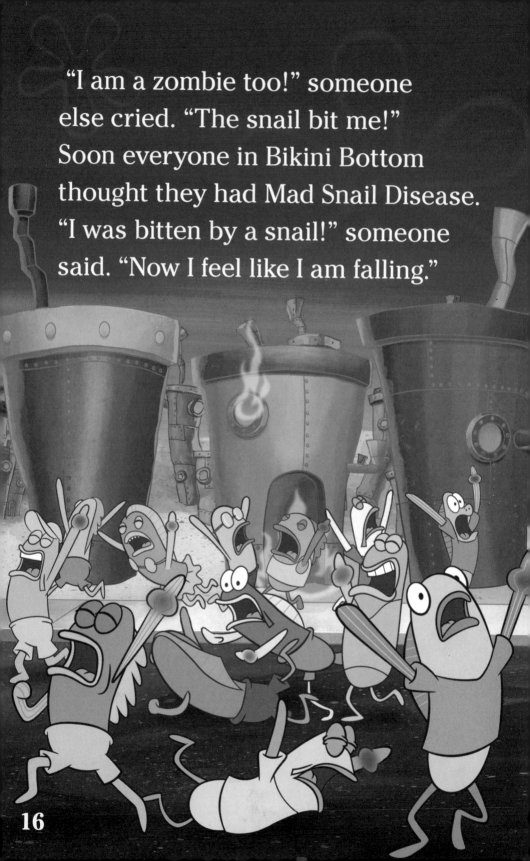

"I am a zombie too!" someone else cried. "The snail bit me!" Soon everyone in Bikini Bottom thought they had Mad Snail Disease. "I was bitten by a snail!" someone said. "Now I feel like I am falling."

"This just in: My ribs feel like they tickle," a TV reporter said. "And I have not been bitten!" "Oh no! It must be spreading through the air!" another man said. "Ahhh!" they all screamed.

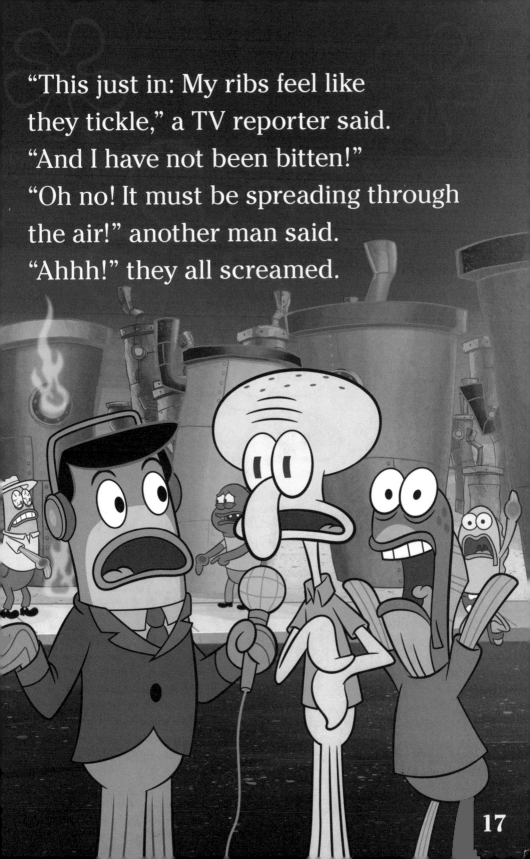

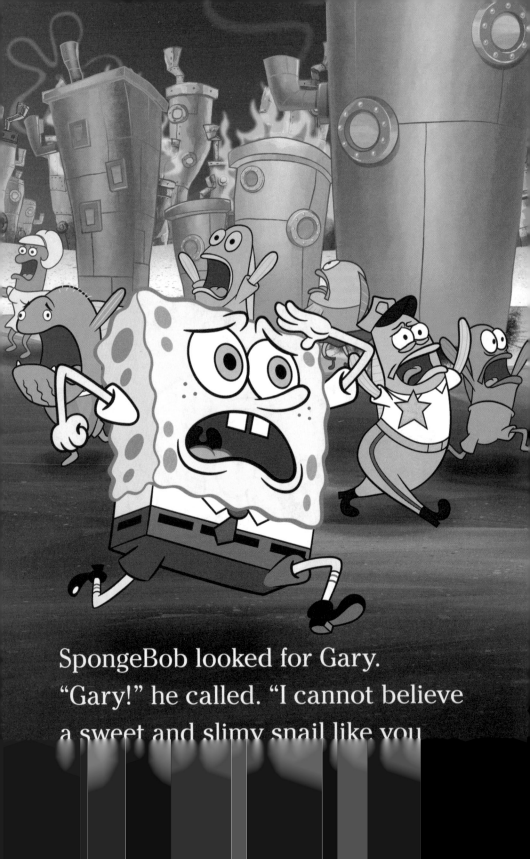

SpongeBob looked for Gary.
"Gary!" he called. "I cannot believe
a sweet and slimy snail like you

"Uhh . . . uhh . . . I am a zombie,"
Squidward said.
"I am here to eat your soft yellow
flesh."

Bikini Bottom was turning into a land of zombies!

"Uhh . . . ," they all moaned.

"Aghhh!" SpongeBob screamed as he tried to get away.

SpongeBob ran to the Krusty Krab,
but the door was locked.
"Let me in, Mr. Krabs!" he yelled.

"Oh, SpongeBob, come in," said
Mr. Krabs. "And bring your
friends too. They look hungry."

The customers would not allow
Mr. Krabs to let anyone else in.
"Stop!" they said. "They are zombies!
They only want to eat us!"

No one noticed that Gary was already inside the Krusty Krab. SpongeBob was happy to see Gary and went to pet him. But the snail was mad—and bit SpongeBob!

SpongeBob gasped. "Gary, how could you?"

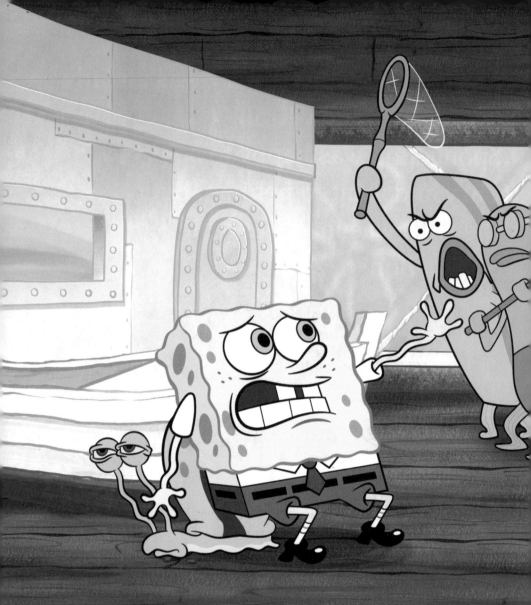

"We have to get that snail before
he bites everyone in Bikini Bottom!"
someone yelled.
"No, don't hurt him!" SpongeBob
cried.

But everyone was eager to see
Gary locked up. "Stop the madness!
Mad Snail Disease ends now!"
Suddenly someone asked, "Wait . . .
did you say Mad Snail Disease?"

The man was Doctor Gill, a snail expert. "I am sorry to tell you all that there is no such thing as Mad Snail Disease," he said.

"But what about my untrimmed toenails? And my ticklish ribs?" "Those are everyday things," Doctor Gill replied. "No one is a zombie!"

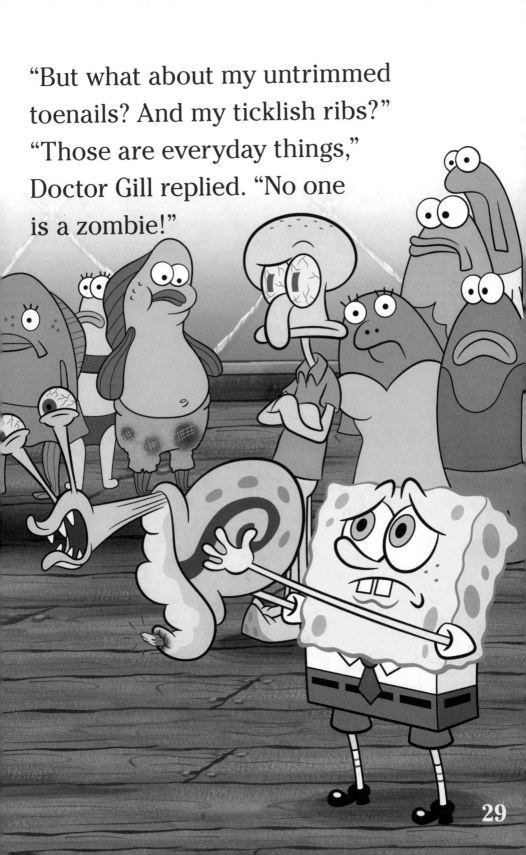

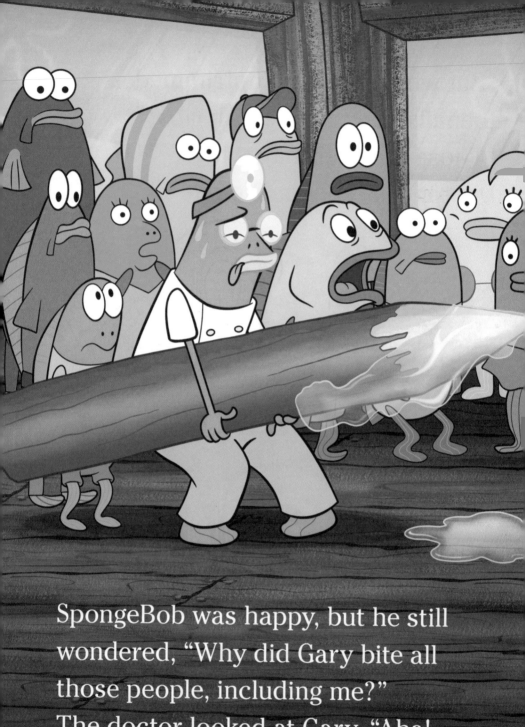

SpongeBob was happy, but he still
wondered, "Why did Gary bite all
those people, including me?"
The doctor looked at Gary. "Aha!
Gary has a splinter in his foot!

That is why he was feeling bad
and biting everyone."
SpongeBob smiled. "Oh, Gary,
I knew you did not have a disease!
I am so glad to have you back!"

"Uhh . . . uhh . . . uhh,"
Squidward muttered.
"Hey, no one is a zombie,"
SpongeBob said to Squidward.
"Yes, I am," Squidward
said. "Welcome to the
Krusty Krab . . . "